Council

Chickenpox

First published in 2010
by Wayland

Text copyright © Jillian Powell
Illustration copyright © Mark Chambers

Wayland
338 Euston Road
London NW1 3BH

Wayland Australia
Level 17/207 Kent Street
Sydney, NSW 2000

Series Editor: Louise John
Cover design: Paul Cherrill
Design: D.R.ink
Consultant: Shirley Bickler

A CIP catalogue record for this book is available from the British Library.

ISBN 9780750261951

Printed in China

Wayland is a division of Hachette Children's Books,
an Hachette UK Company

www.hachette.co.uk

Chickenpox

Written by Jillian Powell
Illustrated by Mark Chambers

WAYLAND

Tilly had chickenpox.
She was itchy all over!

4

"You must not scratch the spots!" said Mum.

Tilly sat down and
read her comic.

"Don't scratch!" said Dad.

Then Tilly did a drawing.

"Tilly!" said Mum.
"Are you scratching?"

So Tilly went to play
a game with Todd.

"Don't..." said Todd.

"I know!" said Tilly.
"Don't scratch the spots."

"I am itchy all over!" said Tilly. "Having chickenpox is no fun."

"I know!" said Mum.
"Let's make puppets!"

She got some socks from the drawer.

Mum got some glue and
Tilly got some buttons.

Together they made
some sock puppets.

"Put them on!" said Mum.
So Tilly put the puppets
on her hands.

"The puppets are fun," said Tilly, "but I'm still itchy all over!"

"But now you can't scratch the spots!" said Mum, Dad and Todd.

START READING is a series of highly enjoyable books for beginner readers. **The books have been carefully graded to match the Book Bands widely used in schools.** This enables readers to be sure they choose books that match their own reading ability.

Look out for the Band colour on the book in our Start Reading logo.

The Bands are:

Pink Band 1A & 1B

Red Band 2

Yellow Band 3

Blue Band 4

Green Band 5

Orange Band 6

Turquoise Band 7

Purple Band 8

Gold Band 9

START READING books can be read independently or shared with an adult. They promote the enjoyment of reading through satisfying stories supported by fun illustrations.

Jillian Powell began writing stories when she was four years old. She lives in a house beside a village church and sits down to write every day. She has written stories and rhymes about dogs, cats, scarecrows and crocodiles as well as children such as Tilly and Todd.

Mark Chambers lives in Lincoln. His studio, where he illustrates, is full of books, drawings and posters and is home to a lobster called Larry!